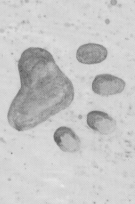

SECRET GARDEN BOOKWORKS
41 Circuit Ave., P.O. Box 1506, Oak Bluffs, MA 02557
www.secretgardenbookworks.com

Publisher's Cataloging–in-Publication
(Provided by Quality Books, Inc.)

Kelly, Sharon L.C.M.,
    Coco's double fun on Martha's Vineyard / by Sharon
L.C.M. Kelly; Illustrated by Alison L. Galbraith
        p.cm.
        SUMMARY: Coco, a chocolate Labrador, vacations on
Martha's Vineyard and discovers a world of double words
and double sounds while visiting all the popular landmark
destinations.
        Audience: Elementary grades
        ISBN:0-9766283-0-9

        1. Martha's Vineyard (Mass.) — Juvenile literature.
2. English language — Compound words — Juvenile
literature. [1. Martha's Vineyard (Mass.) 2. English
language — Compound words. 3. Stories in rhyme.]
I. Galbraith, Alison, L. II. Title.

F72.M5K45 2005   974.4'94
                                                  QBI05-800253

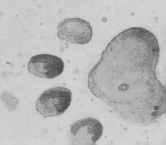

Once upon a time....

    Mama and Papa brought home the *sweetest* Lab they could find.
    Naturally, she had to be one of the *chocolate* kind.
    What a lucky, lucky day it was when they found Coco.
    She's a puppy who makes double fun everywhere they go.

    This story is a celebration of Coco's Vineyard vacation.

Coco's Vineyard Vacation

Double Fun on Martha's Vineyard

Sharon L.C.M. Kelly

by Sharon L.C.M. Kelly

illustrated by
Alison L. Galbraith

Martha's Vineyard!

What a happy, happy island, sparkling in the summer sun!
What a magical place where puppies can make everything double fun!

Mama, Papa and little Coco have a ferry reservation.
They are going to Martha's Vineyard for a double fun vacation.
When they bring a car to the Vineyard, they must reserve a place;
the ferry carries lots of cars, but can run out of space.

As soon as their boat is ready to sail, the crew members say, "Aye, aye,"
and Coco scoots to her favorite spot to watch the waves fly by.
Coco loves to be on deck where she can sniff the salty sea air.
Fifi and Mimi, her island friends, can't wait for her to get there.

Fifi, the pretty white poodle, is very smart and friendly to meet.
Mimi, the cute little schnauzer, is intelligent, funny and sweet.
Look! All the pups are wagging their tails (that's the way dogs grin).
These puppies know that double fun is about to begin.

Oak Bluffs is such a marvelous town.
All their horses go 'round and 'round.
Can puppies ride The Flying Horses?
Don't be silly, that of course is,
"Not Allowed."
While the pups dream of flying horses,
their sad faces draw a crowd.
Fifi, Mimi, and Coco are sad for just a minute.
Then they start to play a game with lots of jumping in it.
"Double Dutch" is the official name
of the puppies favorite jump rope game:

Double, double, this, this,
Double, double, that, that,
Double this, double that,
Double, double, this, that.

Circuit Avenue is a big, big attraction
for puppies in search of good musical action.
Coco and her two best friends love to dance with Rin Tin Tin;
he's the tall, handsome Shepherd with the great big silly grin.
It doesn't help little Toto, to be a movie star,
when he tries to dance cheek to cheek, he can't get very far.

Some puppies like to shake a leg, some only dance so so.
No one keeps up with Mimi, she's a puppy on the go.
She goes gaga over go-go boots, they are her biggest passion.
No one would dream of telling her that they are out of fashion.

At Island schools,
Purple rules!
The friendly Oak Bluffs School has a giant map,
where kids and pups can find doubles in a snap.

Coco, Fifi and Mimi think it would be double fun,
to fly from New York, New York① to Walla Walla,② Washington.
Wouldn't it be fun to see
Baden Baden,③ Germany?
If they started in Baba,④ South America
and ended in YaYa,⑤ in Siberia,
it would take them all day!
It's such a long, long way!

Mama and Papa know smart puppies should never, never go to Dum Dum,⑥ India.
But they sure would have fun, rowing a boat on Lake Titicaca⑦ in Bolivia.
How about a safari trip from Kanda Kanda⑧
to Mala Mala⑨ in the middle of Africa?
The puppies think it would be simply terrific, if they could visit
Nengo Nengo,⑩ Bora Bora,⑪ and Puka Puka⑫ in the South Pacific.

"Show us ♡ Martha's Vineyard ♡ in the County of Dukes County.
You know it's our favorite place to be!"

Some days Coco likes to hang around
at fancy places in Edgartown.
A hot spot for eating well
is the lovely Harbor View Hotel.

Fantastic food really matters,
like couscous and pupu platters.
Where else could Coco go to see
steak tartar and mahi-mahi?

When they ask if you want some sweets,
like pie or cake or bonbon treats,
remember to answer, "Oh yes, please!
I'd like ice cream with M&Ms and Jujubes."

When Coco went exploring by the Gay Head Light,
a little something gave her an itty bitty bite.
She ran over to see the colorful cliffs of clay
and soaked up the sunshine of the glorious day.
Then she needed to do what all puppies do,
so she left the path to go pee pee and doo-doo.

When Coco got back onto Moshup's Trail,
another little something bit her tail!
It wasn't a tsetse fly who played this trick,
it was a teeny, teeny, tiny tick!
So poor Coco,
had to go
to a doctor who
could fix her boo-boo.

BEWARE
OF
DOUBLE
TROUBLE!!

Sniffle
Sniffle

There were lots of sick pets in the vet's waiting room,
but Coco hoped the doctor could fix her boo-boo soon.
The nurse revealed something extraordinary,
"We have a patient here with beriberi!"
Coco tried talking to the Dodo bird,
but the Dodo bird didn't say a word.

Then the nurse started singing happily,
"Chim-chimeny...chim-chimeny...chim-chim...cher-ee."
And then she sang *another* long song,
"When the red, red robin comes bob, bob, bobbin' along."
By the time her songs were through,
the doctor had fixed Coco as good as new.

Some summer days, the very best place to be
is reading and relaxing with your family.
Coco and her Mama love to snuggle up together.
Coco sleeps and Mama reads, one on top of the other.

Mama stays cool and comfy, wearing her favorite flowery muu muu.
Nothing disturbs them until the tiny bird in the clock says, "cuckoo!"

When Coco wakes up, she asks Mama to give her tummy a rub.
Mama whispers, "Dear Coco, you're my sweet little puppy love."

July seventh was a bright, sunny day
for Coco to celebrate her first Birthday.
Her birthday party was a great big surprise,
so her gifts were hidden by a sandy disguise.

Digging and finding became a good game.
What Coco found first was a choo-choo train.
Then she got Ling Ling, a panda bear,
followed by Laa-Laa, who had no hair.

When the game was halfway done,
Coco uncovered a tom-tom drum.
Then she dug up the yellow yo-yo,
and that left one more gift to go.

At last, all the puppies heard her holler.
Coco found the sparkling bling bling collar!

As soon as their sandy game was done,
the pups jumped in for some splashing fun.
Do you want to hear a secret, known by just a few folks?

After swimming, all puppies tell knock-knock jokes!

Home Sweet Home is the place to stay,
if the rain, rain won't go away.
When puppies can't go out to play,
they love to watch movies all day.

Coco piled some videos on the floor
that her Papa got at the movie store.
Gigi was the first movie that Coco chose to see.
When her Papa went to watch *20/20* on T.V.,
Coco learned all the songs they sang
in *Chitty Chitty Bang Bang.*

Even though her pile was tall,
Coco wanted to watch them all.
By the time she finished Bye Bye Birdie,
it was way after 11:30!

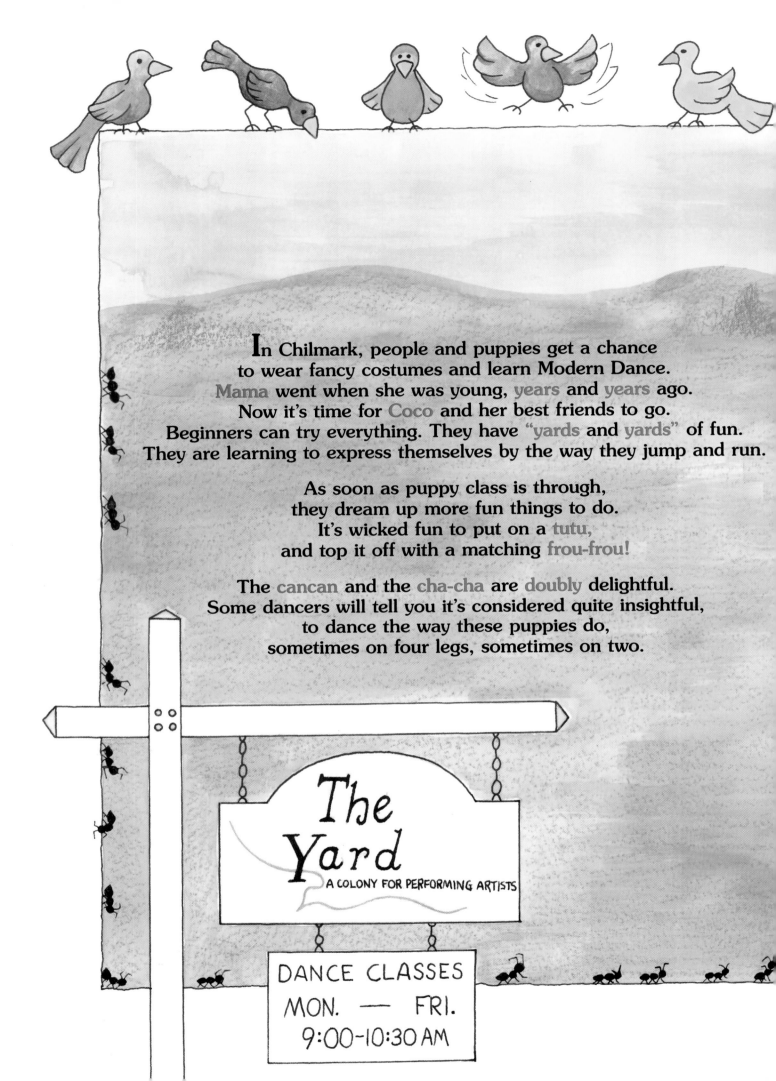

In Chilmark, people and puppies get a chance
to wear fancy costumes and learn Modern Dance.
Mama went when she was young, years and years ago.
Now it's time for Coco and her best friends to go.
Beginners can try everything. They have "yards and yards" of fun.
They are learning to express themselves by the way they jump and run.

As soon as puppy class is through,
they dream up more fun things to do.
It's wicked fun to put on a tutu,
and top it off with a matching frou-frou!

The cancan and the cha-cha are doubly delightful.
Some dancers will tell you it's considered quite insightful,
to dance the way these puppies do,
sometimes on four legs, sometimes on two.

The
Yard
A COLONY FOR PERFORMING ARTISTS

DANCE CLASSES
MON. — FRI.
9:00-10:30 AM

The Dog Show is an awesome event at the Summer Fair.
Every dog on Martha's Vineyard is sure to be there.
Fifi, Mimi and Coco are contestants in the show.
They have been fluffed and puffed and brushed from head to toe.

At the right time and in the right place,
it is O.K. to show off your style and grace.
Competition can be fun,
as long as it isn't overdone.

As you watch the puppy parade go by,
how many breeds can you identify?

— the Chihuahua, Chi Chi
the Dachshund, DeeDee
the Lhasa apso, Lulu
the Yellow lab, Zuzu
the Keeshond, Kiki
the Chow Chow, Charlie
the Pug, Pepe
and the Beagle, Bebe.

Most of the time competing is fun.
Sometimes it's scary for everyone.
The mamas and papas get nervous too,
waiting to see what the judges will do.

There are always cheers for the puppies who win.
Both Fifi and Mimi will get a ribbon!
Mimi's ribbon will be red, and Fifi's will be white,
but the biggest prize of all is still out of sight.

Summer vacation is over, but Mama doesn't want to go.
Papa asks, "Don't you want to come back? We *all* love it here you know."

Coco has everything all figured out. "Mama, we need to pack!
First, people and puppies have to go home, before they can come back!"

Papa yells, "Chop, chop, hurry up, Coco, the boat is here!
Wave 'bye bye' and tell your friends, you'll be back again next year."

See you next summer, Coco! We love you, Coco!

Notes to Parents and Teachers

Aku-Aku is the story of Thor Heyerdahl's explorations on Easter Island, more than 2,000 miles west of the coast of Chile. The island is famous for its huge carved stone figures called moai. No one is really sure about the origin of these statues that stand around the perimeter of the island with their backs to the sea. An aku-aku is a supernatural entity, similar to a personal guardian angel, a secret protector, or an invisible spiritual advisor.

Baba is just north of Ecuador's largest city and major port, in the Coastal Region of this South American country. From Baba it is possible to travel to one of Ecuador's other regions, the Galapagos Islands, where there are few people, but lots of giant tortoises, penguins and sea lions.

Baden Baden (bä´děn bä´děn) is a city in Germany, famous for the healing powers of its thermal mineral springs. It lies just outside the Black Forest, and has the world's fourth largest opera house, beautiful art galleries, museums, and one of the world's largest fleets of hot air balloons.

Beagles were originally bred as hunting dogs. Today they are popular pets, easily socialized with children. They are typically a combination of white, tan and black, with a white tip on the end of their tails. Those tails wag a lot, since these dogs are known as happy wanderers.

Beriberi is a nerve disease characterized by pain in and paralysis of the extremities. It is caused by a deficiency of Vitamin B1.

Bora Bora is an island in French Polynesia. Surrounded by turquoise waters and sandy beaches, the lush vegetation of Bora Bora was created by volcanoes over three million years ago.

Bye Bye Birdie is the story of a rock star who is drafted into the Army. Originally a Broadway show with music by Charles Strause, it was made into a movie in 1963, and featured Ann Margaret in her first movie role.

Chihuahuas (chē wä´ wä) are the smallest of all dog breeds. They are considered to be native to Central America, and typically weigh between 2 and 6 lbs. They have large pointed ears that seem too big for their little heads.

Chim Chim Cher-ee won an Academy Award for Best Song for the 1964 movie *Mary Poppins*. The music and lyrics were written by Richard M. Sherman and Robert B. Sherman. The movie starred Julie Andrews who won an Academy Award for Best Actress.

Chitty Chitty Bang Bang, written in 1964, is the only children's book by Ian Fleming (creator of James Bond). It became a movie in 1968 starring Dick Van Dyke as an eccentric inventor who owns a car that flies. The title song by Richard M. and Robert B. Sherman, was nominated for an Academy Award.

Chow chows existed in Northern China more than 2,000 years ago. They have a lot of fur around the head and neck and their tongues are blue-black. These dogs are known as one-person dogs and they have a tendency to bite strangers when surprised.

Cocker Spaniels were bred to hunt woodcock; that is how they got their name. They have long silky hair, long ears and short tails. They can be black, blonde or particolor. Their dispositions range from sweet and docile to high strung and nervous.

The County of Dukes County consists of the islands of Martha's Vineyard and Cuttyhunk, located south of Cape Cod, Massachusetts. These islands are home to about 16,000 lucky people and their dogs.

Couscous is made from semolina of wheat and water that is rolled back and forth until pellets are formed. The pellets are simmered in boiling water and the result is a light, fluffy, pasta-like dish.

Dachshunds (däks´ hoŏnt) are clever, lively, playful dogs with long bodies, short legs and drooping ears. They weigh less than 30 pounds, are under 10 inches tall and live to be 10 to 12 years old. They love being members of the family.

Dodo birds were clumsy flightless birds in the pigeon family, but about the size of turkeys. They are now extinct. (They were not purple.)

Dum Dum is just northeast of Calcutta, India. Each year over two million people pass through Dum Dum International Airport. If you go there and you don't want to stay in Dum Dum, you might try North Dum Dum or South Dum Dum.

Gigi, based on the novel by Colette, was made into a film in 1958. It is a musical comedy about the romantic life of a young French girl. It won nine Academy Awards, including Best Picture.

Kanda Kanda (can´da can´da) is in the Democratic Republic of the Congo. More than half of the world's 700 mountain gorillas live in the Virunga mountain forests that straddle the border of Rwanda, Uganda and the Democratic Republic of the Congo. Gorillas are gentle, social animals. They eat plants, insects and worms. At night gorillas make a nest on the ground where they sleep. The babies snuggle with their mothers.

A Keeshond (kēs´ hŏnd) is an affectionate, adaptable dog. It is the national dog of Holland, where the breed has been used on river barges as far back as the sixteenth century.

Lhasa apsos (lä´sa ăp´sō) came from Tibet. They were called, "Bark Lion Sentinel Dogs" because they were used as palace watchdogs. They have heavy coats to protect them from the intensely cold winters in Lhasa, the capital of Tibet.

Labrador Retrievers did not come from Labrador but from Newfoundland. They can weigh up to 80 lbs., but are gentle with children. They may be the most popular dogs on Martha's Vineyard, and come in three colors: black, yellow and our favorite, chocolate.

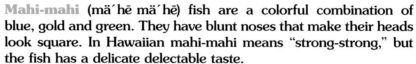

Mahi-mahi (mä´hē mä´hē) fish are a colorful combination of blue, gold and green. They have blunt noses that make their heads look square. In Hawaiian mahi-mahi means "strong-strong," but the fish has a delicate delectable taste.

Mala Mala is one of the ultimate safari locations in the Lowveld area of South Africa. Both the Sabi Sands Private Game Reserve and Kruger Park provide an ideal setting for a wildlife photographic safari. From September to March the Lowveld has an average daytime temperature of 86 degrees.

A muu muu (mōō´ mōō) is a loose fitting dress often worn as a house dress, especially by Hawaiian women. A muu muu is typically made of brightly colored floral fabric.

Miniature Schnauzers are part of the terrier group of dogs. Terriers are very intelligent and high spirited. They are vocal, alert, have a lot of energy and make great watchdogs in spite of their comparative small size, usually weighing 15 to 20 pounds.

Nengo Nengo is an atoll, an island made from coral, in Tahiti. It was uninhabited until 1990, when Robert Wan bought it and made it the home of his pearl farm. The world's largest perfect cultured pearl, known as the Robert Wan pearl, is considered a gem, equal to a precious stone, by the Gemological Institute of America.

New York, New York is one of the world's great cities. People from all over the world come to see the Statue of Liberty, Ellis Island, the Empire State Building, the Metropolitan Museum of Art and the New York Yankees.

Poodles are curly haired dogs, usually white or black. They come in 3 sizes: standard, miniature and toy. Just like humans, they have hair not fur and their hair can be cut in a variety of interesting styles. Poodles are very intelligent and can be highly trained. In France during the 1800's they became popular circus performers, and the breed was sometimes called, "French Poodle."

Pugs are small dogs with wrinkly faces, snub noses and curly tails. They come from China and have clownish loving dispositions. They thrive on lots of attention from their human companions.

Puka Puka is a group of three small islands called motus, part of the Cook Islands in the South Pacific. They surround the lagoon of puka puka which is a rich source of seafood. Puka Puka, known to sailors as Danger Island, because of the hazardous rocks lying outside the surrounding reef, was the first land seen by Thor Heyerdahl sailing on board the Kon Tiki.

Pupu platters are usually a variety of miniature sized servings of food such a fish, beef, chicken and shrimp.

"When the Red Red Robin Comes Bob Bob Bobbin' Along" was written by Harry Woods in 1926, it was in the 1946 film *The Jolson Story* and was recorded by Bing Crosby in 1962.

Steak tartar (also spelled tartare) is a menu item that has lost popularity. The whole dish, once prepared, is eaten raw. Recipes include a combination of ground steak, parsley, worcestershire sauce, onions, pepper, chili sauce, capers, raw eggs and salt.

Lake Titicaca (tē´tē kä´kä) lies high in the Andes Mountains of South America on the boundary between Peru and Bolivia. It is the largest lake in South America and the highest large lake in the world: 3,200 sq. miles and 12,508 ft. above sea level.

Tora! Tora! Tora! When the Japanese bombed Pearl Harbor in 1941, these were the code words, used by the bomber pilots, to inform their commanders that the goal of a surprise attack had been achieved. *Tora! Tora! Tora!* is the title of a film released by 20th Century Fox in 1970.

Tsetse (tsēt´ sē) flies come in 21 different species. They are African, bloodsucking insects that can spread several diseases, including sleeping sickness, to humans.

Walla Walla, Washington was named after the Walla Walla tribe of Native Americans. Explorers Lewis and Clark passed through what is now Walla Walla, where pioneers established a settlement in 1840. Today tourists can visit the site of old Fort Walla Walla, now a museum.

Yaya is in the part of Russia known as Siberia, where winter lasts five months of the year. The Trans-Siberian Railroad makes a stop at the Yaya train station as it passes through four different time zones on its way between Vladivostok and Moscow. The train is a great way to travel long distances.

For additional copies contact Secret Garden Bookworks
866-693-4759 · P.O. Box 1506 · Oak Bluffs, MA 02557
www.secretgardenmv.com

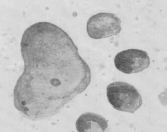

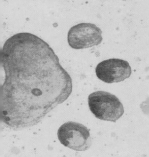